D1028904

Art By Gerome Publishing Co.

P. O. Box 8151, Hampton, VA 23666 • artbygerome@starpower.net • www.artbygerome.com

ISBN: 0-9725790-1-X

Library of Congress Control Number: 2004095719

Printed on acid free paper.
Printed in China

10 9 8 7 6 5 4 3 2 1

Illustrated by Toni M. Thorne
Layout and Design by Image Communications, Charlotte, NC

I dedicate this book to my grandchildren,

Gerome Delshawn Meminger, Satya Dosanjh Meminger,

Marqui Jamal Hunt and Kailani Dosanjh Meminger

and to all my nieces and nephews.

This Book Belongs To

_____

To: OMAR WALKER...
Artfully yours,
Gerome
12/06/04

The Lonely
Little Blue Book

By

Gerome Meminger, Sr.

There once was a lonely

Little Blue Book. The Little Blue

Book lived in the library with his mother

and father. The Little Blue Book was sad and

lonely, because none of the children would

check him out of the library and read

his one and only short story.

The Little Blue Book asked his father and mother when would a little boy or girl take him home and read his one little story? The Little Blue Book's mother and father told him not to worry. His mother said, someday soon, a little girl or boy will come to the library and read all of his wonderful stories, he would one day have inside. His mother said, for now, she would read him a story.

The days and weeks went by. The lonely Little Blue

Book cried and cried. He cried so much he would cry himself

to sleep. Everyday the children would come to the library

and pick out the Little Blue Book's friends but would leave

him sitting on the shelf all by himself. This would make the

Little Blue Book very sad and he would cry.

One day Mr. Joe, the janitor, was cleaning the library, and his broom bumped the shelf. Down fell the Little Blue Book. Mr. Joe continued to sweep the library because he didn't see or hear the Little Blue Book fall.

The Little Blue Book felt the bump on his head.

He got up while in a daze, looked around,

then looked up at his mother and father.

It was naptime so they were still fast asleep.

The Little Blue Book wanted to have some fun so he started playing

and running throughout the library and before he knew it, he

ran so fast that he ran right out the library doors. The Little Blue Book

looked up and found himself outside. He could feel the wind blowing

through his pages, and that made him smile. He was as happy as can

be and decided, it was time to see the world. Once outside, the Little

Blue Book began to run as fast as he could, while jumping and playing.

He ran through the grass, he saw the birds flying, and the trees

blowing in the wind. He looked up in the sky and saw the colors,

blue, green, yellow, orange and red, curved like a bridge.

He was looking at a beautiful rainbow.

The Little Blue Book was playing

close to the woods. He watched two

butterflies that landed on the flowers. Along came

a deer, with long antlers. "Hi, I am called the Little

Blue Book, and what is your name?" he asked the deer.

The deer replied, "My name is Blinker." The Little Blue Book

laughed and asked why was he named Blinker? Blinker said,

"Because in the blink of an eye, I can be gone to safety.

Want to see?" Blinker asked. Then in an

instant Blinker was gone.

As the Little Blue Book went further into the

woods, he saw a billy goat. The billy goat was very hungry and

could eat almost anything, especially paper. The billy goat sniffed

with his mouth watering. He saw the Little Blue Book as a meal and

began to chase the Little Blue Book. The Little Blue Book ran as fast

as his little legs could carry him. He ran faster and faster until

he outran the hungry billy goat. He was

very lucky and frightened.

Tired and hungry, he stopped and found

himself lost in the woods. He began to cry.

As the Little Blue Book cried, he heard something

moving in the woods, it was a hunter in the woods

hunting. He heard the lonely Little Blue Book crying.

The hunter asked the Little Blue Book,

why was he crying?

The Little Blue Book told his story to the hunter. The hunter was

very sad about the Little Blue Book's story. He picked up the Little Blue

Book and began to write. He filled so many pages in the Little Blue Book.

He wrote about all of his many adventures around the world. These

stories included ferocious lions, tigers, bears, tall mountains, fast

moving rivers, and the many countries he had seen. The Little Blue

Book grew bigger and wiser as the hunter wrote and wrote.

After the hunter finished writing in the Little Blue Book, he took

the Little Blue Book back to the library. The Little Blue Book's

mother, father and all the kids were so happy to see him

back home. He began to dance on the floor with joy because

now he has so many stories inside to be read. The Little Blue

Book was back home and on the shelf with his mother

and father. His mother said he had grown so much

from being on his journey.

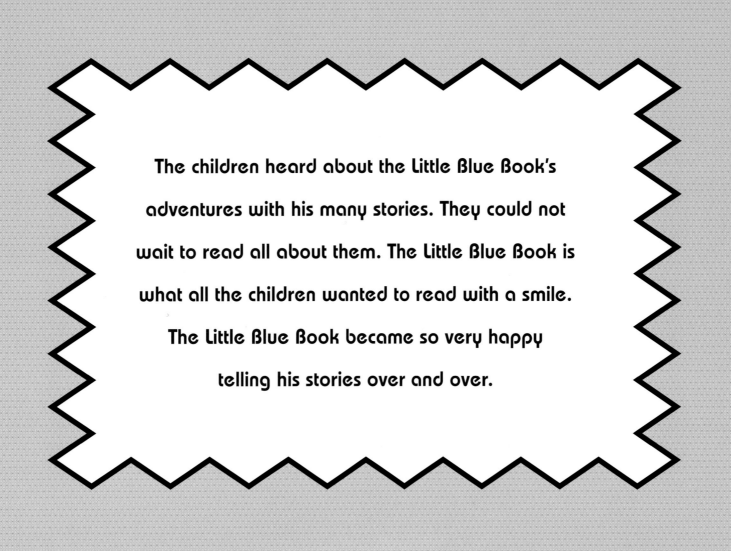

The children heard about the Little Blue Book's

adventures with his many stories. They could not

wait to read all about them. The Little Blue Book is

what all the children wanted to read with a smile.

The Little Blue Book became so very happy

telling his stories over and over.

Now the children go to the library looking for the lonely

Little Blue Book that is now a happy Little Blue Book.

THE END

(PSSST!!!!! Don't forget the other little

lonely books...They want to be read, too.)

ABG
PUBLISHING